ALVIN
THE PIRATE

ALVIN THE PIRATE

by Ulf Löfgren

Carolrhoda Books, Inc./Minneapolis

One day Alvin went to the beach to search for buried treasure. He brought his big shovel with him. "If *I* were a pirate, where would I bury my treasure?" Alvin wondered. He searched and searched. Finally he found a spot that he thought would be perfect for burying stolen treasure.

So Alvin began to dig.
It was hard work. He dug
and dug until suddenly his
shovel hit something hard.
"I bet it's a treasure chest
filled with gold," thought
Alvin. "I bet pirates buried
it here." He began to
dig faster.

"Wow! I found a treasure
chest, and I didn't even have a
map." Just then Alvin heard
someone shout, "Captain Alvin!
Captain Alvin!"

Alvin looked up and saw a whole shipload of pirates coming toward him. "We've found your hat and pistol, and the ship's cat too. Someone hid them in a barrel on the ship."

"Over there, Captain, look. Oscar Bluenose is waving your hat and pistol over his head. Come on! Let's dig up the treasure and sail off. How 'bout it, Captain Alvin?"

"How do you know my name? I don't know yours.
And why are you calling me captain?" Alvin stammered.

"Shiver me timbers! You haven't forgotten your old
mate Sniffy Sinbad. And you can't have forgotten you're
the captain of our ship. The other pirates are a whole new
crew, so it's no wonder you don't know them. That's
Oscar Bluenose, Hilmer the Foot, Ferocious Ferdinand,
Napoleon Washtub, Anton the Terrible, Snook the Chin,
Simon Sideburns, Homer the Horrible, and Ghastly
Gustav."

Now that Captain Alvin knew what was going on, he was ready to take charge. "Dig up that treasure chest," he said in his best captain voice. Then Alvin whispered to Sniffy Sinbad, "I can't remember the name of my ship."

"Shiver me timbers!" cried Sniffy. "It's one thing to forget your mate, but to forget your ship! It's the *Seawitch*."

"Oh yeah—I mean aye," Captain Alvin replied.

It wasn't long before the pirates had dug the treasure chest out of the ground. They dragged it down to the water and loaded it onto the boat.

"Seaward ho! To the *Seawitch*," cried Captain Alvin.

"Aye, aye, Captain."

When they were all aboard the ship, Alvin climbed onto the treasure chest. "Long live Alvin, our pirate captain," the pirates chanted.

"Let's set sail and rove the seven seas," cried Captain Alvin.

"Aye, aye," the pirates shouted. It was high time they got on their way.

The *Seawitch* had just set sail when the pirates heard Charlie Cannon shout "Ship ahoy!" from the crow's nest. "Heaven help us—that's the pirate ship *Pale Death*, our deadly enemy. And they're coming toward us at full sail!"

"Everyone to the cannons," Captain Alvin ordered. "We'll smash the *Pale Death* right into the sea."

"Aye, aye, Captain," cried Sniffy Sinbad. "But we're all out of cannonballs and we don't have any bullets for our pistols."

"What do you mean we're all out of cannonballs and bullets?" asked Captain Alvin. "I've never heard of a pirate ship being out of cannonballs and bullets. What are we going to shoot with? I bet the *Pale Death* has more than enough cannonballs and bullets."

"Aye, you're probably right," said Sniffy Sinbad. "But we have melons and grapefruit and apples and oranges on board. We can use those instead."

"I guess that will have to do," said Captain Alvin. "But it seems funny somehow—melons, oranges...."

But the *Seawitch* pirates were lucky. The *Pale Death* was out of cannonballs and bullets too. In fact, the enemy pirates had only tomatoes to fight with—and tomatoes are quite harmless, as everyone knows.

So the battle raged. Melons and apples and oranges and tomatoes flew through the air. Suddenly, Captain Alvin realized he was hungry. "These green apples taste pretty good," he said happily.

But Sniffy Sinbad knew they shouldn't let their guard down yet. "Captain Alvin, Captain Alvin," Sniffy Sinbad shouted. "The *Pale Death* is coming closer—they're going to come aboard! What should we do?"

"We'll have to draw our swords and sabers," said Captain Alvin.

"Oh, no. We left our swords and sabers at home," groaned Sniffy Sinbad.

"Then what are we going to fight with?" demanded Captain Alvin. "What kind of pirates are you, anyway, leaving your swords and sabers at home!"

"Aye, well, we have lots of cucumbers and sausages on board—we can fight with those," Sniffy Sinbad suggested.

"Then arm yourselves, mates," Captain Alvin ordered. "Look over there! The pirates on the *Pale Death* have forgotten their swords and sabers too. They're fighting with asparagus and carrots and bananas. Ha ha ha!" Captain Alvin began to laugh.

But he shouldn't have laughed so quickly.
The *Pale Death* was ready with a surprise attack.

"Help!" cried Sniffy Sinbad and Ghastly Gustav. "They're pouring huge buckets of salad dressing on us. We're going to get all sticky."

"Shoot them with whipped cream and raspberry syrup," shouted Ghastly Gustav. "Then they'll be sticky too."

Captain Alvin had a better idea though. "Halt!" Captain Alvin shouted to the pirates on the *Pale Death*. "I want to talk to your captain, Captain Blood-Blackbeard."

The one-legged, one-eyed Captain Blood-Blackbeard stomped onto the *Seawitch*.

"After all this fighting, we're all pretty hungry," Captain Alvin said. "Instead of battling, let's get together and make a salad for dinner. We've got cucumbers and tomatoes and carrots and asparagus and sausages and thick, creamy salad dressing."

"Hrmm, aye, that is a good idea." Captain Blood-Blackbeard was hungry too.

"Then we can have fruit salad for dessert. We've got bananas and oranges and melons and grapefruit and lots of green apples. And we have whipped cream and raspberry syrup," offered Captain Alvin.

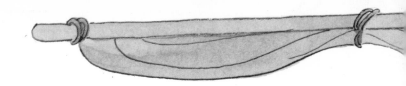

What a feast! Everyone ate lots of salad with thick, creamy salad dressing. The fruit salad and the big buckets of raspberry syrup were finished to the last drop. Full and happy and tired, all the pirates fell asleep.

But the pirates from the *Pale Death* only pretended to
be asleep. They got up quietly, seized the sleeping Captain
Alvin, and sneaked silently back to their ship.

The next morning, Captain Blood-Blackbeard used his wooden leg to poke Captain Alvin awake. "Well matey, we're not going to make you walk the plank, I promise you that," grinned Captain Blood-Blackbeard. "No. You're going to take a little trip off the seesaw." And Captain Blood-Blackbeard laughed a great roaring, horrifying laugh.

Three pirates lined up on the poop deck as Alvin sat down on the seesaw. "See that you all jump together," ordered Captain Blood-Blackbeard. And those pirates came down on that seesaw so fast and so hard that Alvin flew through the air and...

...out over the ocean in a terrifying flight, dropping both his pirate's hat and his fine pirate's pistol...

... until, at last, he landed right where he had
left his old cap and his shovel. "It's just as well,"
thought Alvin. "I was tired of being a pirate anyway."

Library of Congress Cataloging-in-Publication Data

Löfgren, Ulf
    [Albin sjörövare. English]
    Alvin the pirate / by Ulf Löfgren.
        p.   cm.
    Translation of: Albin sjörövare.
    Summary: Young Alvin sails off with a band of pirates, who seem to
think that he is their captain, and they all engage in a food fight
with the crew of another pirate ship.
    ISBN 0-87614-402-4 (lib. bdg.)
    [1. Pirates—Fiction.] I. Title.
PZ7.A48   1990
[E]—dc20   89-37477
                                                       CIP
                                                        AC

Manufactured in the United States of America

1   2 3 4 5 6 7 8 9 10 99 98 97 96 95 94 93 92 91 90

DATE DUE

JUL 1 2 1999		
JUL 2 7 1999		
AUG 1 1 1999		
AUG 2 5 1999		
AUG 2 1 2000		
OCT 1 0 2000		

DEMCO 38-297